This book belongs to:

To Paul, for being my rock and
helping me to follow my dream – SQ

Quarto is the authority on a wide range of topics.

Quarto educates, entertains and enriches the lives of
our readers—enthusiasts and lovers of hands-on living.

www.quartoknows.com

Author: Susan Quinn
Illustrator: David Creighton-Pester
Editor: Ellie Brough
Designer: Victoria Kimonidou

Copyright © QED Publishing 2018
First published in the UK in 2018 by QED Publishing

Part of The Quarto Group
The Old Brewery
6 Blundell Street
London N7 9BH

A catalogue record for this book is available from
the British Library.

ISBN 978 1 78493 940 3

Printed in China

Max
and Bear

Susan Quinn

Illustrated by David Creighton-Pester

Bear loved Max.

Max loved Bear.

Every day they had
adventures together.

And every night Bear would tell
Max wonderful bedtime stories.

One day Max and Bear were flying kites with Dad.

Suddenly, a gust of wind pulled the kite out of Max's hands.

The string wrapped around Bear and the kite carried him up into the sky.

Bear was flying!

Bear flew off towards the woods,
far away from Max and Dad. But then...

"Help!" cried Bear as he tumbled **down,**

down through the trees...

...before landing
in a bush with a
bump.

Bear's head hurt and he drifted
off into a strange sleep.

He dreamt about
Max having tea
without him,

sitting quietly in
the bath instead of
chasing pirate ships...

...and staring sadly out of the window.

But when he dreamt about Max missing his bedtime stories...

...Bear woke up!

It was dark as he peeked
out from under the bush.

There were strange shadows on the
ground and the wind made funny noises as
it whistled and whooshed through the trees.

And there was a
strange thumping
noise getting closer,

and
closer,

and
closer.

"Who's there?" cried Bear.

"Sorry we frightened you," said Rabbit,
who was with Badger and Mouse.

"Are you lost?"

Bear told them about the
kite carrying him away.

"I must get home," he cried.
"Max won't sleep without
my bedtime stories!"

"We'll help you," said Badger.
"Do you know the way?"

"It's too dark,"
said Bear.

"Then we'll wait for
Moon," squeaked Mouse.

"Hop on my back," said Badger
when Moon appeared.

Badger and Rabbit ran through the forest,
with Moon's silvery glow lighting their way.

"This is fun!"
squeaked Mouse.

"We're nearly home!" shouted Bear when they
reached the clearing where Max had flown his kite.

"Thank you for helping me," said Bear when they arrived home. "But how will I get inside?"

"That's easy!" said Rabbit, thumping on the door.

Rabbit, Mouse and Badger hid as Bear waited...

Dad opened the door
and Max rushed out.

"Bear!" he cried, "I thought
you'd flown away!"

Dad scratched his head.
"How did Bear get here?"

"Bear can do
anything!" said Max,
hugging him tightly.

That night, Bear told Max the best bedtime story ever. It was about flying through the sky, being lost in the spooky woods and meeting brilliant new friends.

And Max drifted off to sleep, happy that Bear was safely back where he belonged.

Next Steps

Discussion and Comprehension

Ask the children the following questions and discuss their answers.

- What did you like most about this story?
- Why was Bear frightened?
- Why did they wait for Moon?
- Can you think of a word to describe how you would feel if you lost something that you cared about?

Character Description

Ask the children to look in the book and name the different types of animals. Give each child a piece of paper with a circle drawn in the middle, surrounded by four boxes. Label the boxes: how did your character help solve a problem? What do you know about your character? What does your character look like? Why did you choose this character? Ask the children to choose one of the animals, draw a picture of it in the circle and write a sentence in each box. Ask them to read out their character descriptions.

Make a Kite

Give the children large sheets of paper cut into kite shapes. Give them strips of tissue paper or crêpe paper to make a kite tail. Provide coloured crayons, shiny paper, safety scissors and glue sticks so that they can decorate their kites.